Writing Right

by Cassandra Baker

Illustrated by Noor Moiz

WATERTREE PRESS

Writing Right

Schoolbell font created by Font Diner, licensed under the Apache License, Version 2.0

Published by Watertree Press LLC

PO Box 16763, Chesapeake, VA 23328

https://www.watertreepress.com

Notice of Liability

The information in this book is distributed on an "as is" basis, without warranty. While every precaution has been taken in the preparation of this book, the publisher and author make no claim or guarantee as to its correctness, usefulness, or completeness for any reason, under any circumstance. Nothing in this book should be construed as an attempt to offer or render a medical opinion or otherwise engage in the practice of medicine. The information in this book is not intended to be a substitute for professional medical advice, diagnosis, or treatment. Always seek the advice of your physician or other qualified health provider with any questions you may have regarding a medical condition. Moreover, the publisher and author shall have no liability to any person or entity with respect to loss or damages caused or alleged to have been caused directly or indirectly by the information contained in this book.

Publisher's Cataloging-in-Publication Data

Names: Baker, Cassandra, author. | Moiz, Noor, illustrator.

Title: Writing Right / by Cassandra Baker ; illustrated by Noor Moiz.

Description: Chesapeake, VA: Watertree Press LLC, 2020. | Summary: A young boy learns to work through his struggles with dysgraphia through perseverance, help from his mom, computer resources, and occupational therapy.

Identifiers: LCCN 2019948867 | ISBN 978-0-9911046-3-5 (pbk.)

Subjects: CYAC: Agraphia–Fiction. | Learning disabilities–Fiction. | Writing–Fiction. | Academic achivement–Fiction. BISAC: JUVENILE FICTION / School & Education. | JUVENILE FICTION / Disabilities & Special Needs. | JUVENILE FICTION / Health & Daily Living / General.

Classification: LCC PZ7.1.B35 | DDC [E]–dc23

Library of Congress Control Number: 2019948867

About the Author

Cassandra Baker is a high school student from Virginia who joined the Girl Scouts of America when she was ten years old. Cassie decided that she would earn the Gold Award, the highest award in Girl Scouts. Her drive was to follow in the footsteps of her grandfather, father, and two brothers who had all earned their Eagle Scout award in Boy Scouts.

Cassie decided to write and publish a children's book that would help kids cope with the learning disability dysgraphia. She also wanted to provide resources for parents and guardians who assist these children. Cassie grew up with family members who were affected by dysgraphia, this experience influenced her decision to write a book for this often overlooked population.

She would like to thank all those who helped throughout this journey, especially her family, friends, and Girl Scout Troop. Special thanks to Occupational Therapist Robin Hull for serving as her Gold Award Advisor.

Cassie is proud to present her Girl Scout Gold Award Project: *Writing Right.*

Hi, I'm Noah.

I have a ton of awesome ideas. I'm pretty good at describing my ideas out loud but writing them down is hard.

My handwriting is not exactly the greatest, and Mom says I have trouble moving my thoughts from my head, to my hand, to the paper. I just think that I don't know how to write right.

I watch the kids in my 3rd grade class, and they get their work done super fast. They're like writing robots.

We have Warm-up Writing Wednesdays, where we have to write sentences that answer questions about our lives or about something we've learned in class. Some kids get them done in what seems like five seconds, while I'm sitting there still working on number one or two.

I get a little upset when this happens because I don't understand how they do it.

One time I balled up my paper and threw it on the ground. I just couldn't figure out how to make my pencil listen.

I wish I could invent my own writing robot that would write whatever I tell it to.

My teacher, Ms. Smith, is really nice, but she sometimes gives us work to do at home.

One time we had to make a poster about ourselves to show to the class. I wanted to make mine look cool. I spent forever working on it, but I just couldn't get it to look the way I wanted.

Mom tried to help, but I got so mad that I yelled at her and ripped my poster in half.

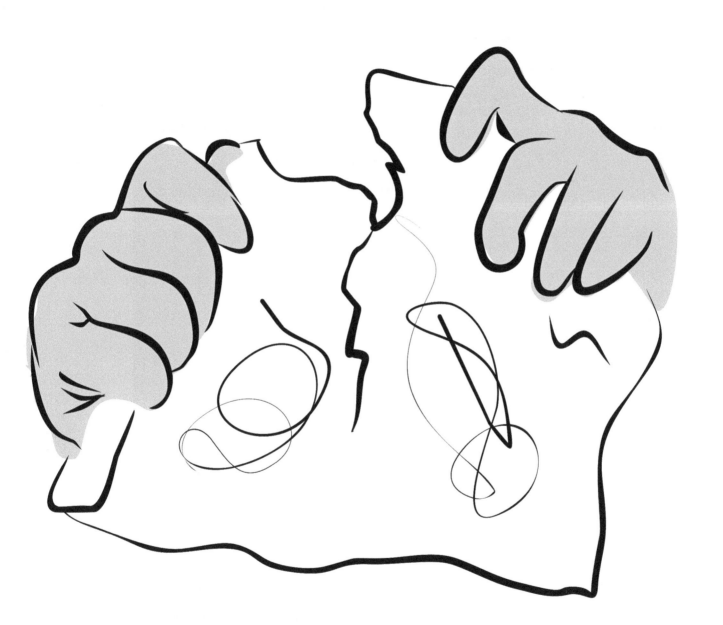

After the poster meltdown, Mom started having meetings with Ms. Smith. I got a little worried that I could be in trouble, but when I asked her what they were meeting for, she told me that they were talking about ways to make school easier for me.

I thought not going to school anymore might solve the whole problem, but Mom shut that idea down fast.

Mom and Ms. Smith had a different plan. They decided that I could use Mom's computer to help me with my homework.

At first, I was a little confused. I didn't understand how a computer would help me write better. But after Mom let me try it out a bit, the plan made sense. Instead of having to write out those difficult letters, I could just push a button, and ta-da, there it was!

At first it took me a while to get words typed out, so Mom showed me a website that helped teach me how to type better.

After a bit of practice, it started getting easier. I could type a few sentences in the time it used to take me to write a word or two by hand. And the best part was that it was super easy to read!

At home there was no more messy handwriting for me. All my letters were crystal clear and I could put all my cool ideas on paper.

I even wrote my own story about an army of robotic dinosaurs that take over the world.

Homework was easier now, but not everything can be done on a computer.

To help with the times that I did have to write by hand, Mom sent me to an OT. She told me that it stands for Occupational Therapist.

I didn't really know what that was, so I wasn't a big fan of the idea at first.

It turns out that my OT, Ms. Natalie, is really cool. She does exercises with me that are supposed to make writing by hand a lot easier.

We do fun things like pull "aliens" from theraputty, cut shapes with scissors to make pictures, and use tweezers to pick up shells and sea creatures from sand. We also draw a lot of figure eights and other curved shapes and lines with chalk, scented markers, and bright colored pencils.

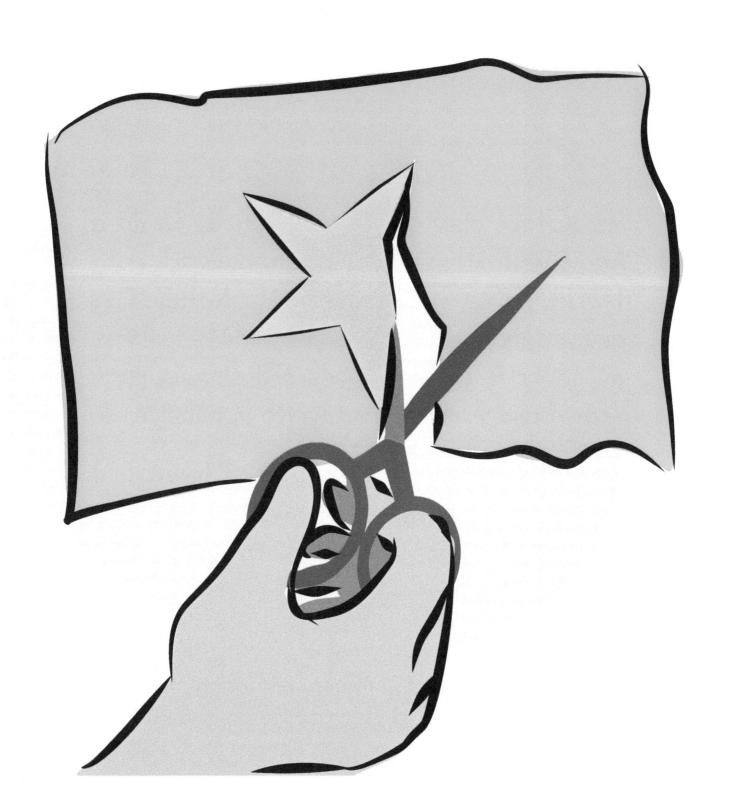

Ms. Natalie also gives me practices to do at home with Mom. Unlike the homework my teacher gives, the activities Ms. Natalie gives are pretty fun. We do dot-to-dots, color my favorite super heroes and dinosaurs, draw hand turkeys, and write in cursive.

Mom and I practice every day at home and the more I do each practice, the easier they get.

Since I've been doing so well with the practices, Ms. Natalie wanted me to try doing some of my homework without Mom's computer. I wasn't sure if I could do it at first, but after I tried a few times, I realized that I could!

Now I do a lot of my homework on my own, without the help of the computer. Ms. Natalie was really happy when I told her.

Although I still don't have the best handwriting ever, it's gotten better.

Ms. Smith told Mom that they don't have to meet anymore because I've gotten so awesome!

I like school a ton more now too.

Last week, Ms. Smith assigned another poster project. This time we needed to describe something we wanted to do in the future. Mine was about my writing robot idea. The poster turned out great, and I even drew a picture that wasn't half-bad.

I never thought that I'd be writing right.
Mom is really proud of me and said that I
should be too, and you know what?

I am!

What is Dysgraphia?

Dysgraphia is a learning disability that affects a person's writing and fine motor skills. Those with dysgraphia often have poor handwriting and may struggle with:

• Hand eye coordination
• Expressing themselves on paper
• Holding writing utensils correctly
• Writing within line spaces
• Using tools such as scissors or tweezers

There is no single cause for dysgraphia, but in many cases, it stems from neurological issues. The parts of the brain that influence a person's fine motor skills are impaired in one way or another, causing difficulty when performing certain tasks. Many with dysgraphia also have other coexisting issues. These can include dyslexia, attention deficit hyperactivity disorder (ADHD), sensory issues, vision issues, or other learning disabilities. Caregivers should look out for additional issues.

How can it affect a child?

A child with dysgraphia may face both physical and emotional difficulties. The physical limitations can stem from the development of the child's hand muscles. Children that have dysgraphia often hold their writing utensils incorrectly. A child who does this consistently can cause interference with the proper development of the muscles in their hand. It can also result in physical pain, poor handwriting, and frustration.

Children can get frustrated when something doesn't go their way or fails to meet their expectation. The inability to complete a basic task, like writing or cutting with scissors, can cause a child to get angry or sad. They may make excuses to avoid fine motor work. They can get down on themselves and feel a sense of failure. Difficulties can also cause feelings of embarrassment if they are unable to perform as well as their peers.

Where to seek professional help

There are multiple ways to seek professional help for dysgraphia. Many schools have professional Occupational Therapists on staff who are trained to help children with dysgraphia. In the U.S. a parent or guardian has the legal right to request that a child be evaluated for learning disabilities under the Individuals with Disabilities Education Act. All public schools are required to comply with these requests. The procedure can vary by state but if the evaluation confirms dysgraphia your child may be eligible for professional services provided by his or her local school. Private Occupational Therapists are also an option and can often work one-on-one with a student outside of school environments. In addition to professional help, a child will progress faster if a caregiver is also working with the child at home. Caregivers will ideally partner with their child's OT to reinforce new skills at home and encourage practice.

Helpful resources

• *Hand Function in the Child: Foundations for Remediation* by Anne Henderson and Charlane Pehoski

• *1001 Pediatric Treatment Activities: Creative Ideas for Therapy Sessions* by Ayelet H. Danto and Michelle Pruzansky

• Understanding Dysgraphia in Children: Written Expression Issues at https://www.understood.org

• Understanding Dysgraphia - International Dyslexia Association at https://dyslexiaida.org/understanding-dysgraphia

• Learning Disabilities Association of America - Right to an Evaluation of a Child for Special Education Services at https://ldaamerica.org

What can be done at home?

One way dysgraphia can be worked on at home is by making sure that a child is holding the pencil correctly. This can be done by demonstrating and practicing proper finger placement, or, for children that find it especially difficult, there are special pencils and pencil aids that can be purchased online or at an office supply store that help encourage a proper grip.

Another way to help at home is to be very encouraging. Help them to get through their assignments by validating their efforts and providing frequent breaks. There are also plenty of easy exercises that can be done at home.

Finding a Grip

Teach the child to hold a pencil correctly as seen in the diagram below (any of these grasps are generally considered acceptable). Attempt to find which of these holds is most comfortable for the child. Once your child finds a comfortable grasp, see if they can repeat the grasp after setting the pencil down. Repeat this until the grasp becomes automatic. If the child struggles, try adding a pencil grip writing aid. There are many different pencil grips available for purchase online or in stores that sell office supplies.

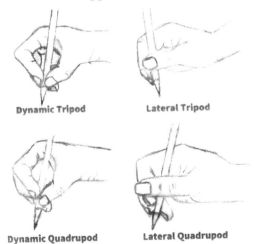

Dynamic Tripod   Lateral Tripod

Dynamic Quadrupod   Lateral Quadrupod

12 At Home Tips and Exercises

1. Practice holding a pencil using one of the four methods shown in "Finding a Grip." Decide which is most comfortable.

2. Write with different types of instruments. Use pencils, pens, and markers of varying widths when writing.

3. Draw or trace simple figures or shapes on a piece of paper.

4. Spread out multi-colored beads, candies, or other small objects and use the thumb and index fingers or tweezers to pick up and sort the objects by shape or color.

5. Write in cursive or in some form of connected letters. Cursive is often easier than print.

6. Repeatedly squeeze an object by clenching the fist and then releasing. The object could be a stress ball, balloon, blanket, pillow, etc.

7. Sculpt, mold, and squeeze materials like dough or clay.

8. Poke two holes in a small piece of cardboard and thread one shoe lace, string, or ribbon through both holes. Tape it down to a surface and use it to tie knots or bows.

9. Use a finger to trace out words on paper before writing them out or have the child draw letters on your back and then guess what letter or word was written.

10. Use scissors to cut paper into different patterns such as straight lines, zig-zags, or waves.

11. Practice completing dot-to-dot assignments.

12. Trace hand prints on paper, and, if desired, design them into fun hand turkeys.

Lightning Source UK Ltd.
Milton Keynes UK
UKHW050947080721
386821UK00005B/154